The Twelve Days of Christmas

ILLUSTRATED BY JOHN O'BRIEN

Boyds Mills Press

For Tess

Publisher Cataloging-in-Publication Data
Main entry under title.
The twelve days of Christmas/illustrated by John O'Brien.—1st ed.
[32]p. :col. ill. ; cm
Summary: Humorously illustrated edition of the traditional song.
HC ISBN 1-56397-142-9 PB ISBN 1-59078-086-8
1. Christmas music—Juvenile literature. [1. Christmas music.]
1. O'Brien, John, ill. II. Title.
783—dc20 1993
Library of Congress Catalog Card Number 92-73990 CIP

Published by Boyds Mills Press, Inc.
A Highlights Company
815 Church Street
Honesdale, Pennsylvania 18431
Printed in China

First edition, 1993
First Boyds Mills Press paperback edition, 2003
The text of this book is set in 14-point Galliard.
The illustrations are done in pen and ink, dyes, and waterc

10 9 8 7 6 5 4 3 2 HC
10 9 8 7 6 5 4 3 2 1 PB

On the first day of Christmas,
my true love gave to me...

A partridge in a pear tree.

On the second day of Christmas, my true love gave to me...

Two turtle doves

On the third day of Christmas, my true love gave to me...

Three French hens,

two turtle doves,
and a partridge in a pear tree.

On the fourth day of Christmas,
my true love gave to me...

Four calling birds,

three French hens,
two turtle doves,
and a partridge in a pear tree.

On the fifth day of Christmas, my true love gave to me...

Five golden rings…

four calling birds,
three French hens,
two turtle doves,
and a partridge in a pear tree.

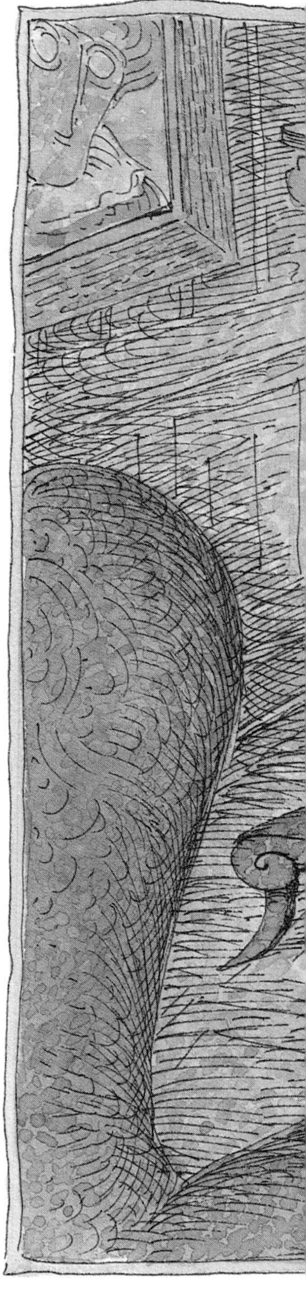

On the sixth day of Christmas, my true love gave to me...

Six geese a-laying,

five golden rings,
four calling birds,
three French hens,
two turtle doves,
and a partridge in a pear tree.

On the seventh day of Christmas,
my true love gave to me...

Seven swans a-swimming,

six geese a-laying,
five golden rings,
four calling birds,
three French hens,
two turtle doves,
and a partridge in a pear tree.

On the eighth day of Christmas,
my true love gave to me...

Eight maids a-milking,

seven swans a-swimming,
six geese a-laying,
five golden rings,
four calling birds,
three French hens,
two turtle doves,
and a partridge in a pear tree.

On the ninth day of Christmas,
my true love gave to me...

Nine ladies waiting,

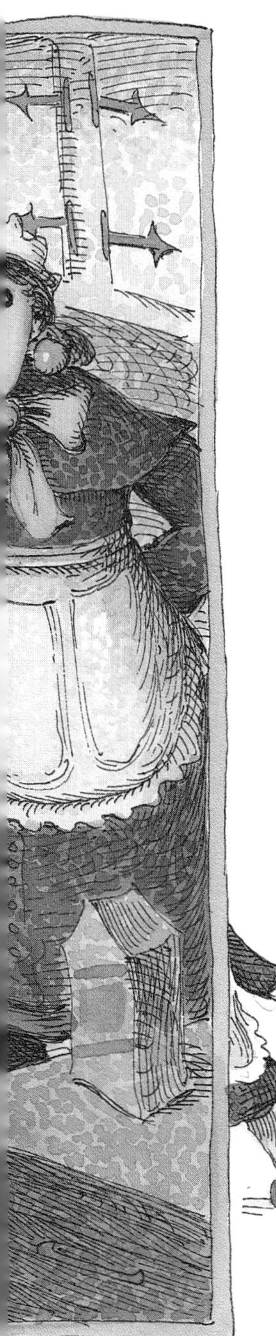

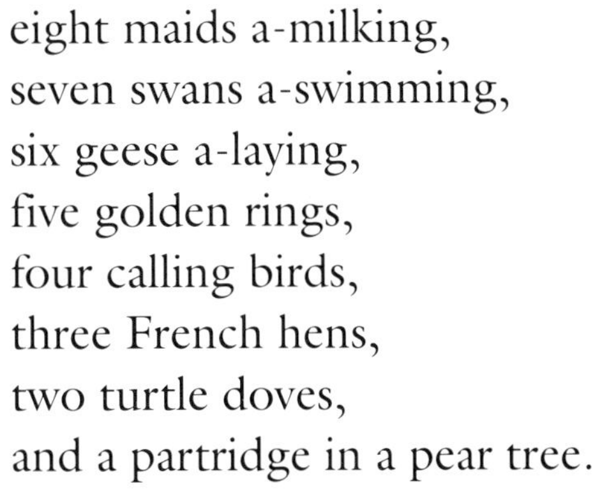

eight maids a-milking,
seven swans a-swimming,
six geese a-laying,
five golden rings,
four calling birds,
three French hens,
two turtle doves,
and a partridge in a pear tree.

On the tenth day of Christmas, my true love gave to me...

Ten lords a-leaping…

nine ladies waiting,
eight maids a-milking,
seven swans a-swimming,
six geese a-laying,
five golden rings,
four calling birds,
three French hens,
two turtle doves,
and a partridge in a pear tree.

On the eleventh day of Christmas, my true love gave to me...

Eleven pipers piping,

ten lords a-leaping,
nine ladies waiting,
eight maids a-milking,
seven swans a-swimming,
six geese a-laying,
five golden rings,
four calling birds,
three French hens,
two turtle doves,
and a partridge in a pear tree.

On the twelfth day of Christmas,
my true love gave to me...

Twelve drummers drumming,

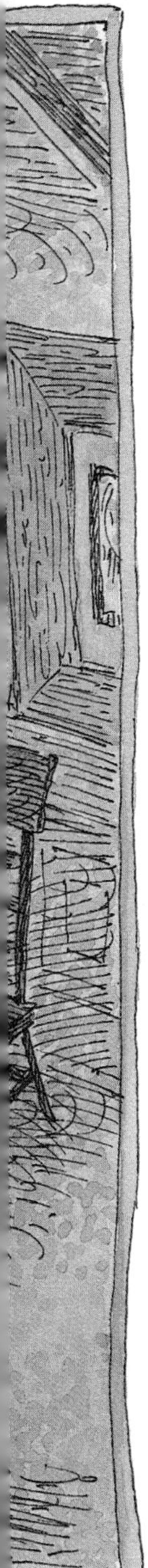

eleven pipers piping,
ten lords a-leaping,
nine ladies waiting,
eight maids a-milking,
seven swans a-swimming,
six geese a-laying,
five golden rings,
four calling birds,
three French hens,
two turtle doves,

and a partridge in a pear tree.

NOT
HOME